# Love They Said

Love takes on many shapes, some of
them less than pleasant although we
don't like to think about it

Else Cederborg

authorHOUSE®

*AuthorHouse™ UK Ltd.*
*500 Avebury Boulevard*
*Central Milton Keynes, MK9 2BE*
*www.authorhouse.co.uk*
*Phone: 08001974150*

*First published by AuthorHouse    11/10/2011*

*ISBN: 978-1-4670-0168-7 (sc)*
*ISBN: 978-1-4670-0169-4 (e)*

*We are being taught that love is the most important event in our lives so of coarse most people are looking for it. However, love may both be a wonderful experience and a most devastating one. Also it may pose dangers to the heart and psyke like nothing else because nothing hits as hard as love when it goes wrong. As if that wasn't enough love also poses real physical danger to first and foremost women.*

*The danger comes from the other side of "love" which turns it into violence or maybe even worse. Also some power games are sort of distilled into the realm of love.*

*Still, we love LOVE, i.e. the idea of passions, eternal tenderness, adventure and full understanding in the one we love. This craving for love may even turn some os us into genuine love addicts. Some feel that a day without love is wasted. And what if one is the object of another individual's passion, but doesn't love this person oneself? Isn't that a most harrowing experience? Well, still it's called "love"...*

# Contents

# Poems

# I Heard My Name In the Wind

Yes, called out like a flourish of trumpets
not something that goes unheard
something one may miss or ignore
no, absolutely not
resounding in vibrant tones it made itself heard

Was it a dream sent out by my own soul?
A forgotten message from me to myself?
Something I should remember, but had forgotten?
Or was I summoned by someone?
Maybe put under an obligation

I don't know, a riddle formed in my life
no clues came to me, no solutions
only some questions: Am I on the right track?
Did I do what I was meant to do?
Could I be guilty of crimes I don't know of?

My ears are tuned in to trumpets
however, they listen in vain
still, the flourish is there
somewhere in the blood at my temples
in my heart - in what's me, a flourish sings out

# Uprooting Dead Love

Fragments of dead love
fluttering in the wind
still, in our hearts a memory lives
yes, that feeling lives in both of us
however, what must be done
will be done at once
sharpen your dagger as I do mine
cut your shackles and fly free

# To Share and to Share Alike

King Salomo knew how
"Cut him in half," he said
one child, two women contesting

The same drama goes for another scenery
one man, two loving women
who shall win that prize?
Maybe winning will not be WINNING?

# Fire

Fire-love, cuts like a knife in butter
it's obvious I'm out for slicing
no escape as it cuts into me
laying bare layer by layer
this is my list of feelings
of loves and hatreds
out for everyone to read
engraved in my flesh
eternally scorching my heart and soul

# My Universe

My Universe came first
I tagged along far behind
newborn I didn't claim it
for ages and ages
Why would I? Secrets are secret
Mine revealed itself one night
It clutched its heart and yelled
"Wake up! I'm yours!"
Embarrassed at the theatricality
I took one look and woke up
there it was, my Universe
the setting for my loves
for my everything

So this is me, I thought
suddenly dismayed at this chaos
this for and against
forward and backward
I stilled my dissatisfaction
suddenly possessed by
what I possess - my universe

# Eyeless

This blindness wears me down
I grope my way in darkness
touching forbidden items
stepping on all the toes there are
and all this for being blinded by love

Not seeing reality is hazardous
it kills in dark times
one gets too smug about security
the blow to one's head comes from within

# Steal Your Way

What made me abstain from stealing?
Why didn't I catch that thief?

I might have stolen from you
what you stole from me
but no, I didn't
my regrets are too late
now you steal from someone else

The prison is my heart
but you escaped
neither thief nor prison guard
I lose out to both

# Elastigirl

Elastigirl knows how to bend like a rubber cane
she puts her body in positions quite unknown on planet Earth

Elastigirl turns heads all the time
she goes from normal into freak in one split second

Why, when the Earth is still sailing in Space?
nothing wrong in being limber, but for whom?

Does it get her a free ticket to visit the moon?
Is she happy when she ties a knot on herself?
Maybe she sees her lover sailing through Space
one knot and then another
untying for each other

# What Is This?

What is this tingling in my soul?
Who asked it to break its state of hibernation?
Not I!

Everything was so tranquil, but now, up and around
wants this, wants that, wants everything
Lie still, rest, sleep, be quiet, I say
It just flashes lights at me, dances and sings
and I, being exasperated, sigh like grandmother
when the grandchild grows up and craves LIFE ...

## Talkative

What happened?
A volcanic eruption in my heart
a waterfall from my lips

Feelings turned into words
all of them tumbling down imaginary slopes
alarming bystanders as they fall
Oh, don't be alarmed, I shout
they are strong, made from iron
can't get hurt
some of them even bounce

# Silent Rain

Standing still, not thinking
not speaking
but engulfed in my feelings of love

The rain drops fall upon my face
they make their way down my cheeks
talkative like burning tears
but I have no ears to listen
quenched by the inertia of life they die on my tongue
Actually I suck them in, one by one
each a short lived tale of love and life

# Snakes in the Grass

How beautiful they are
rubber bands made of diamonds
all of them snakes
innocent killers coiling along

Very adept at what they do
touch and be seduced by silk
what a surprise to see it move

Handfuls of snakes
but symbols of what?
Slaughtering murderers?
Slowness, dumbness, hatred?

No, of life itself, shedding
changing, growing new
eternally by the law of Nature
watch the snakes and dream of new loves

# Snake-Love

My miraculous snake-body lives
it's dancing to rhythms of its own
no dragging along of this many-coloured band
living the life of venom and dances make agile
a killer-machine tickling the furry prey
easing it down in a deadly embrace

This is what a snake's love is about
hunting, mesmerizing, devouring
maybe that's all there is in the land of love
dance, tickle, embrace and devour

# To Love A Snake

Snakes don't go steady
they slither away
venomous and lethally beautiful
poison in a sneaky, silky package
slimmer than slim, gets in everywhere
leaves their marks as kisses of death

To love a snake isn't wise
they dance too well
only they forget your steps
all they want is to sway you
yes, sway you to their rhythms
to dance you into oblivion

# Snake-Princess

Venom in my veins made me kiss snakes
what I did was to wrap myself around them
to drag them to my world and to feed upon them
not fair, no not in the least, but convenient
snake-princess I was called, but I was not
no, more like a snake demon, full of venom
spitting words out with a split tongue
calling it "The Ultimate Truth"
oh yes, that's me being me in Snakeland

# Predator

Predatory thoughts roam the streets
sniffing out the victims to be
these predators have daggers for teeth
hooks for hands and fire for bodies
merciless they stroll down the streets
everything set out for the kill that's called love

# Love

True love
the one in fairy tales
the one hand in hand with passion
that's the dream

However, the brother of dreams are nightmares
just like in dreaming tenderness
passion, love
but meeting harshness
maybe still stay loving
that's the formula for Hell on Earth

Maybe you should grow wise and harsh yourself
outlove your love, although living in tears?
None of it easy, all of it human and seen before

# I Am

I am:
my blood
my heart
my eyes
actually, each part of me is me
still, I might live without these parts

No arms, no legs
maybe blind
or disfigured by wars or illnesses
when I grow old I may have lost most of me
still, I'm perceived as me

If so, what constitutes the me of me?
Am I a faceless shadow or a rock hard mirror image?
Something fluent or something carved in rocks?
A voice speaking out or a secret feeling only known to myself?

Tracing the lines of my face I don't find me
recalling events in my life I meet a part of what is me
however, one's memory is a joker out to tease
other people's memories may call mine a liar

Fluttering in and out of looks, of memories I'm all and nothing
everything and nothing at the same time

Locking eyes with my mirror image I see
I even perceive and feel a me in me
the one made of feelings and wishes
almost impossible to quench this craving is me
long lived it hollers "Respect me, I'm ME"

# I met you

That said I want to make it clear
that everything was made clear to me, kiss by kiss

Now I know that I know much, but never all there is
and now all riddles were blended into one:
How come that I don't have to know everything to be loved?
To be perfect in soul and body?

# Loving A Ghost

Turning to face you isn't enough
I need to touch you and to see you
invisible as you are
my face may be close to yours
but my hands and mouth don't find you
you swim in aether, or so they say
to see you means closing my eyes
expanding my vision to see even more
the features of your face reappear
kept young forever in this revival in my mind
lovable you, forever who you were

# Moving Freely

Moving hands and feet
free, just like in water
in air
in Space
or maybe in a dream
maybe not even my dream, but yours

Moving lips and body
and even more

Moving a soul
maybe not only mine, but also yours
or maybe only yours
or only mine
what matters is the movement
the pulsations in body and soul
yours or mine
pulsating life making us move

# Puppy Love

This handsome guy is youth incarnate
fourteen and beloved
that's what he hates the most
the noisy love by aunts and grandparents
cooing over him, calling him "cute"
being kissed by Granny he shrinks
in a moment he grows back in time
suddenly a toddler in the assertive age
the less they know, the better
they never guess his many secrets
his life is not what they think
this man-boy is the lover of many
a baby he is not, but he is a father
his hobbies are more like crimes
but still, he is so very, very cute

# Tyrant Heart

Her wayward heart turned tyrant
scorched in the furnace of love
still it clamours for passion
for fires, for flames
even for pyres

Leaning against the flames it nearly expires
stupid one, almost scorched beyond repair
still, the clamour is there
"love, and all of it for me," it shouts
somewhere the echo stutters "--- me-me-me"
yes, a me-me-me-love is for the take, not for giving

# Waves of tenderness

Did you feel it, all over you body, like a storm?
These waves of tenderness were invisible hands
let loose as kisses and caresses
turning your skin into a blanket of sensors
each of them reporting a new secret place
one which also aches for storms and tenderness
silence isn't part of the pact between us
this is a time of heavenly sighs and talkative places

# Electricity

Brushing past you, electricity in the air
sparks, invisible, but very perceptible
like little whiplashes turning on the heat
sets the blood galoping
our paleness suddenly turns rosy-red
our cheeks a flag of defiance?
no more fugitives in our own lives?
Who knows, we don't

# All That's You

Looking at you, loving you dearly
taking you in, all that's you, body and soul
recognizing you for what you are

I know a secret that belongs to everybody
to forget this secret is human, most do it
still it's the law of the living:
this which is you is all of this single moment
accepting this sanctifies this special moment
this situation is washed away by time
as is this status in looks and feelings
you as you are now are a passing image
it's not to be found a year or ten from now
but this moment I take you in and love you
your beauty, this seemingly solid frame
you are you and still, you too must obey the law
the law of the living

# Bodily Body

This is my castle
derelict and abused
yes, this is my inherited castle
it came to me through a line of generations

Once set out to be beautiful and strong
now, very picturesque
like ruins in paintings
inhabitor: one

# Self-Hatred

Born he was
and loved
everyone adored him
except one: He hated himself

"A knife in his heart
(make it red-hot and turn it around)
let the blood run ..." he hizzed
the man in the mirror listened
and smiled
This hatred came from nowhere
(or so it seemed)
and what's more, it ran its own course
the blood that he drew never was his
but it sure was spilled

# A Body At War With Itself

My hands lead lives of their own
wishes and desires rule them
as they do with my entire body
for instance, my hair wants to cover you
to wrap you in Samson-strong ropes
my arms want to embrace you
to hold you lovingly tight
My heart plays havoc with my brain
it wants to shed love and tenderness
my brain's wisdom is overruled by the heart
no-no, it says whatever was done is forgiven
the brain is sizzling with plans of its own
none of them altogether loving and forgiving
a body at war with itself
loving and hating at the same time

# Fate, You Joker

I came to think
or I *came* to think
maybe I came to *think*
No other reason for my birth
or just something that happened

And what about love?
It happened or it *had to* happen?
Fate, or just a coincidence?

Well, I was grabbed by my hair
my heart was torn out
turned around and pinched alive
I think that both happened and was FATE ...

# Up And About

Once more
up and about
dragging years and days behind me like a half-shed cape
leaving a sticky trail like a snail's
I don't deserve it, but I survive
even this and that rotting in my private cellar

Still, I may ask: So this is life
- or is it LIFE?
Never mind, the postman proves my existence
letter by letter by letter from somewhere
I don't know the sender though
never mind, the letters find an adress
somehow that must be mine
somehow I must be me

# Liar

Sadness rules loves and lives
look out it says
this is not worth the while
lying soothsayer yelling out truths
none of them TRUE

# Masters of Darkness

In the end all of it blending into lights
that's what I believe in
however, light may be weaker than darkness
Maybe all of it blending into one big black nothingness?
If so, what then?
Shall we grow eyes like moles who don't see much?
Or maybe eyes like the big cats?
Those light-footed creatures, made to kill
darkness holds no problem to feline murderers
they see what it is and penetrates it to see what it hides

Maybe the mole doesn't even see the darkness
still, it masters it, living a life embedded in blackness

Which ability will be ours, the deep knowledge or the blissful unawareness?
Which one was born with us as part of our souls?
Mole or tiger? Both of them masters of darkness

# A Knot for Your Memory

How easy it is to forget the facts of life and love
perhaps one should make a knot of oneself to remember
what shouldn't be forgotten
or perhaps one should un-knot all those false reminders of "facts"?

By now I know that not even all of me can bring you solace
nor give you all that you need
to give oneself, but not be the right gift, what a curse
no doubt about it, that knot hurts the most

## Like A Fly In A Glass Jar

Trying to - yes, what?
I see him and he sees me
this is a flirt like many before
I know full well this situation
in the deepest of my knowledge
it rings out, over and over:
"rein lust, don't let it loose
or let it loose at a cost?"

The glass jar resounds with claws
scratching as I cave my way out

# Springtime in Winter

This is it, my hands grow soft
my heart is mellowed by you
what is it called when icy winds turn warm?
When ice sculptures turn living flesh?
Could the proper word be Love?

Maybe it's just Spring and nothing but that
something passing and not for keeps
still, a gift from somewhere

## That Loving Feeling

She wanders in green
although the street is brown
nonetheless, her soul moves in a meadow
she feels the flowers tickling her feet
summer fragrances tease her mind and heart
forgotten, but sunny memories erupt once again
in the cold wind of Autumn she feels warm
even though the icy air carresses her cheeks
easy does it and slowly it pierces her breast
if a heart could smile hers would laugh
it doesn't shun the ice-fingers of Autumn
no, walking in meadows brings strength
the heart melts the ice, bringing back the warmth
she doesn't even feel it, humming a love song
still living in a sunny world of green

Make a list, yes, make a list
get a grip on this, will make it go away

# Escaping

Such nimble feet, they almost dance
walking like a fire cracker
all of a sudden everything is speed and movement
normally she feels her way, eyes closed, ears alert
no sounds are allowed, when feet trail invisible paths
some of them leading to love
others leading away from Cupid and all his machinations

Her heart beats the rhythms of her walking
Stay with him – no leave – stay – leave it says
nothing she does can still its yelling
exhausted she stops, taking in the landscape
to her surprise she finds herself on a suspension bridge in Space
up there with the stars she feels her feet growing into roots

# Patience

There is a rare feeling called "patience"
pinch it, make it suffer, it woun't revenge itself
maybe it rejoices, but most often suffering is all it can
this drop of celestial tears cries its way through time
yes, the laments sounded for centuries
still, pinch it and it sings like a chime
this rarity never made a stir, never warred
not many met it outside legends and myths

That is, turn that second cheek and there it is
brought out just like a rose bud grows into a flower

# Aileen W.

Cheerful and lethal
lying all the time
murderous with a smiling face
you shot them, Aileen
how did your revenge taste
did you feel in command
paying back those who paid you?

You let them torture you into this
doing more to them than they did to you
you became the scum you fought
besides, your death lasted too long
year by year you died
growing into a monster, little by little
so unfair to one who was born an angel

# Moulded in the Paradise-form

Like marzipan, like velvet or silk
maybe moulded in the Paradise-form
like Eve, like Adam
maybe with a touch of the snake
soft as the softest material
alive with pulses
one human frame
alive

# Love for Sale: African Prostitute In Europe

What a gift, wrapped in laces
even a talkative one
tick-tock it said when unwrapped
definitely meaning something else
maybe something like "leave me alone"
difficult to hear, but not a happy sound
this gift is not for sharing, it was robbed
it's loot, tick-tocking away in anger
somewhere the desperation sits
maybe in the eyes or in the foreign tongue
or maybe in the photo of the children
this gift is a mother, and this mother is a gift
but not to her kids, left in Africa
robbed of her they look at us, wondering

# My Lips Didn't Find You

My hands found you in the darkness
my mouth reached for your lips
electrical flows set the air ablaze

All that was before I woke up
hugging empty space

Yes, I forgot that you weren't here
Yes, I'm an idiot, forgetful and silly
but even the air tasted of you

# The Famous Actress

Celebrity all over her face
even an unparalleled, exotic beauty
this is she, the famous one
Ophelia, Cleopatra, Maggie and Martha
all those famous women rolled into one
when she cries 100 women cry
when she moves 100 women move
but what when she can't move anymore?
Do they die with her?
No, on the contrary, she lives with them

## Actions Like in the Movies

Calamity, unbound rage
useless to stop fires, except within
this cost lives, nine in all
carried from the house in body bags
gone forever, ogled by bystanders
disappointment at the bags
sensational tragedies made private
Mr. and Ms Everyman don't like that
some poke the site of the fire
turning charred pieces of wood
hoping to find sensations of death
something for discussions when bored
all want more, more and more
The Grim Reaper in a cage
the fire itself in a bowl
and the pyromaniac back in the house
all of it action like in movies

# Awakening

Awakening, supple like a saturated tigress
shredding the sleep off in a little paw-dance
I reach for the loft, waving all four paws
Otherwise: Do I do what I do so often?
Oh yes, being me I certainly **am** me
so I edge towards you, still deep in sleep

Not planning anything, but doing it
a fire cracker couldn't wake you more thoroughly
alert is not the word, but I savor your attention

# Allurements and Mistakes

What were those allurements?
No reason to sustain delusions
Tentacles held me, may have been my own
however, someone lured someone

Too late to stem against those allurements
when dragged along, past the stop signals
never even pausing for reflections
hailed by ghosts of sad mistakes of the past

# Stopping

Take my blood
I don't need it anymore
my heart just stopped beating

dip your living feet in it, taste it
let your warmth meet my coldness
will do you good to bathe in blood
you, an innocent Dracula
marked down in my blood
you were bloodied by love

# Combustion

Desire, as defined by your eyes
dug deep, but came uncalled
how did it grow in frozen earth?

Little by little smallest sparks were born
tuned in on the subject of combustion
amuzed and unbelieving
even when my heart caught fire

# Femme Fatale

An alluring femme fatale
well known to poets and desperate men
famous writers redesigned her life
they turned it into a myth
a tale of love and cauldrons of desire
nothing but that and always caught in the act
a love machine, tick tocking like a watch
worshipped for causing men to dream
enwrapped and adorned in myths of love
however old age disrobed her
but still, tick tocking like a watch
a victim to the myths of herself
she tried to stir her cauldrons of desire

# The Box of Fun

So this is the famous box of fun
I ordered it, expecting to find it full of items
instead it came here empty except for sounds
I turned it upside down, but empty it was
the sounds were buzzings, birds' song, rain drops
and much more like babies laughing, whales singing
but still, no items, nothing to put up on shelves
no items for exhibiting or bragging about
I nearly tore it apart looking for SOMETHING SUBSTANTIAL

On finding nothing I phoned the company and a voice said:
"Don't you like the sounds, don't they give you fun?"
I put down the receiver, looking at the box of fun
actually, it was long since such fun in my world
I couldn't help smiling as I opened it once more
the sound of happy babies and puppies came floating
nothing more fun than that

# Doll's Faces

Doll's faces everywhere
all of them cracking into craters
no shyness of revealing the plastic
they go pop-pop like popcorn
Where did they come from?
An invasion from Outer Space?
A mask modelling your soul into tritenes?
How come? What happened?
I don't know, must have fallen asleep ...

# Games of Love

Wasn't it agreed upon, our declaration
independence was the name
or was it dependence?
Didn't we find way to new dimensions
or am I mistaken once again?
Perhaps, what we had, was ghostly plays
trite and silly games, all called love
none of them quite what we thought

Maybe the games of love made rules
came true, forgotten, but still alive
Memories kept them, feelings fed them
together the grew into ghostly giants
here to haunt us forever

# The Passion of Lady Chatterley

The lady Janes of this world go a'hunting
when the Chatterley-woman speaks out
passions as festival games make rock hard meetings
beloved by Mellors the velvety dripstone caves blossom

No more Mellors, you say, the gamekeeper died?
The game started by the keeper of love lives on
ghostly it pops up, scaring those who should adore
Nature's masterpiece in functionality and eloquence

And Constance? The keeper of the Jane above them all?
Oh, she lives, talking with many mouths, but do they listen?
Languages change, one million words in English now
Living in Babel confuses Lady Jane, some words escapes her

# Boa Proof

Eat my kisses, devour my lips
but first of all, savour my pulsating skin
vibrating to your rhytms
set astir by you and your touch
working myriads of pulses

One of us is coiling the other
to the point of making bodies boa proof
no one doesn't know the power of lips
not much speaks as well as lips kissing lips
maybe except hips hugging hips

# Pyres of Desire

Fire-points make my skin tingle with you
igniting at touch they turn into a bonfire
this heat from another heat brings me down
yes, down to worship the power of fires

These fires roam my blood and flesh
they burn, transforming our love
we stand on pyres made of desire
consumed by flames

## To Hear Love Speak

Often nobody listens
no one understands
to understand a heart's language takes more than ears
only true hearts speak it and those are all too rare

# Obligations

Another obligation, even before breakfast
overwhelmed doesn't cover my feelings
more like shocked and awed
this really is an obligation, a not too easy one

From now on I have to take care of something vulnerable
something very alert, too fragile by far, and breakable
some obligations grow on one, some are just too much
this one is both, and I feel tied down in the reins of love
that's the magic of small ones, tyrants in a world of love
this one is your heart, tick-tocking to my rhythms

## Anything But Tears

No in-depth like this
sky high or knee deep
but into what?
Fluids of any description
streaming like tears
being anything but

## Paradise Love

You turn your face upon me
The lucidness encompasses me in radiance
each of my feautures, each atom a sign
my soul goes to play, running happily with yours
playing in Paradise, living love as it should be

# Devour, Eat And Spit Out All Surplus Bones

Yeah, maybe my metabolism will show you love
Is that what fills your head with dreaded images?
Carnivore, cruel teeth biting into living flesh?
And then all those screams ...
Your screams, your blood, and your flesh

Maybe too much, Witches' Sabbath in
fear and destruction, called love, but painful
even to contemplate

But then, when I serve myself as your dish
will you then eat until you're full?
Will your love be our dishy dessert
the pudding for fulfillments?

# A Body of Lips

Come, kiss me all over
don't leave out one particle that hunger seeks
I'm tasteable as I turn to meet your cravings
however none of my limbs lack a mouth of its own
each part of me contains a couple of lips
sucking in the lips of each part of you

# Body to Body

This meeting in air
floating in and out of each other
silhouettes in laces
embracing what's left by the fire
that revived my tired soul
body to body with Eternity

# Dreaming of New Dreams

Sudden kisses
like lightning, born in fire
how did that happen
I didn't call for love
No, I walked in fields of poppies
dulled asleep by their magic
dreaming placid dreams
even dreams of other dreams
all in a happy blur, not made for waking

# Obsolete Love Configurations

Different strokes altogether
changes in obsolete love-constellations
may take forever

# Kissing A Croc

An entire cave full of teeth
too many to keep inside
yes, that mouth is too loose
too slack, and much too false

Chewing and processing
that's what it does, mostly to people
no one is safe for those croc's teeth
pearly white killers of reputations
tabloids they are called
rotting meat between the teeth

# Passionate

Her wayward heart turned tyrant
scorched in the furnace of love
still it clamours for passion
for fires, for flames
even for pyres

Leaning against the flames it nearly expires
stupid one, almost scorched beyond repair
still, the clamour is there
"love, and all of it for me," it shouts
somewhere the echo stutters "--- me-me-me"
yes, a me-me-me-love is for the take, not for giving

# Trust me

I'm trustworthy
I reflect
no judgements, only reflections
sometimes I get bored, but still I reflect
that's when they don't dare to look me in the eye
that eye is open, non-judgemental
the cruelty they see in me is nothing but blankness
I reflect

They call me "mirror" and some hate me
to be trustworthy is being cruel they say
dreaming of dark rooms
invisibility
charming light by candle sticks
I'm none of that, I'm the truth
the one who says "no love for you, Miss Hippotamus"
or "too many sixpacks for being one"
somehow that seems to make me guilty
judgemental
cruel
that's the nature of THE TRUTH ...

I am silver and exact. I have no preconceptions.
Whatever I see I swallow immediately
Just as it is, unshadowed by love or dislike.
I am not cruel, only truthful-
The eye of the little god, four cornered.
Most of the time I meditate on the opposite wall.
It is pink, with speckles. I have looked at it so long
I think it is a part of my heart. But it flickers.
Faces and darkness separate us over and over.
Now I am a lake. A woman bends over me,
Searching my reaches for what she really is.
Then she turns to those liars, the candles or the moon.
I see her back, and reflect it faithfully.
She rewards me with tears and an agitation of hands.
I am important to her. She comes and goes.

Each morning it is her face that replaces the darkness.
In me she has drowned a young girl, and in me an old woman
Rises toward her day after day, like a terrible fish.

# Short Stories and Fables:

# Loves and Crimes

The outcome of sunny weather and birds' song may very well be a bundle of joy. At least that was how I came into this world. The sun and the heat made my parents careless as to clothes and the birds' song may very well have turned their heads. Even though they were practically strangers, I appeared as an unexpected present nine months after one of their very first dates.

Big surprise? No, not exactly as my Mom and my maternal grandmother had done everything there was to be done to get rid of me before I was born. It's strange to think of now, but they really hated me before my birth, but afterwards they shovered me in love. As did my paternal grandmother when she learnt about me. She, being very strong and domineering, even saw to it that I was adored by that elusive figure, her son, i.e. my father. Without her he wouldn't even have seen me, I'm sure.

After his death in a mysterious shooting accident and my divorce from Eric I moved in with her, simply because I lacked a place to stay and she was of an age that made it important that someone would look after her. Not that she ever was sick because she wasn't. Never-ever as much as a cold, but there was her almost incessant complaints of obscure ailments. It was a bit annoying, but I would rather have a hypochondriac for grandmother than someone who really was ill.

"How are you?" I asked her every morning and her answer was always the same: "Oh, I'm sure the Good Lord will free me off my shackles and release me very soon". At first I simply didn't understand what she was talking about, but having heard this over and over it dawned upon me that to her life as such was something one ought to leave as fast as possible and the means to do so was to pray for a speedy death. However, God was the only one who really could take off those "shackles" and when that happened one wasn't quite sure where the destination was set for: Up or down - Paradise or Hell.

I couldn't help laughing a little at this thought, but only when she didn't notice. She was old and she wanted to get relief for her ailments and I was young so I only wanted to have fun and to LIVE. That is, I also wanted her to have fun and to live because I really loved her. She had saved me from my Mom's family who consisted of criminals and psychopaths. You may wonder at me saying this, but it's true: My poor, loving and very vivacious Mom ended up a crack-feind, her brothers went in and out of jail, one of them served a sentence for robbery and murder. As to their kids then they were just as bad and I abhorred all of them. At this point my paternal Grandmother - Olympia del Marco Stuart as was her grandiose name - was the leading star in my life.

We were a lot together, but she always wanted me to date and to find "a better man than that Eric, such a (mumble, mumble, mumble) .... guy" I never told her that I was the unfaithful and bad one in that marriage. Frankly, I didn't have the heart to do so, her being such a Grand Lady.

The only one who knew was my Mom. She was never impressed by my marriage, but Olympia she admired. "A very strict lady," she said, "and so very rich ...."

"Rich? She is always complaining of being so very poor."

My Mom laughed so she dropped her cigarette and started to cough. I helped her to regain her breath and she continued: "She is loaded, lots of money, her husband was rich, ..."

I shook my head as I didn't believe it.

"Oh yes," she went on, "Olympia was clever and I bet she hides her money in the house ..."

That last comment made my hair stand on end: "No-no," I said, suddenly quite worried, "I would have found it by now. After all, I help her cleaning the place." This part of the conversation was like a flaming danger alert because, with my Mom I was in the company of a genuine gangsters' Moll. However, she comforted me when she saw how worried I was, but as I left, her eyes had that special glint that I had seen before when she was planning.

Only two days later Hell broke loose. Oh yes, and the Devil himself was my eldest brother, Robbie, a sleek, good-looking guy, charming and not in the least trustworthy. A "yes" from him might mean anything from "no" to "Timbuktu" and this special day he wanted a "yes" from Olympia. "Do you have money stacked away?" he asked and she was supposed to say "yes", but Olympia being Olympia said "no". That was when it got nasty - and that was when I got back home.

I was supposed to go to my maternal Grandmother that day as she was feeling poorly, but she had cancelled our appointment over the cell phone so already on my way to see her I returned back home.

As I opened the door I, for once, didn't yell out my usual greeting of "Hello, dear", but stopped in my tracks and listened. Everything was so silent that it was uncanny. Not even Olympia's little dog was to be heard. I didn't like it one bit so I took off my shoes and tiptoed into the kitchen. Here I found blood in the sink and a lump of meat of some kind. I poked it with a knife and felt so nauseated at recognizing it as a severed thumb that my stomach started to hurt. Somehow Olympia had lost one of her thumbs. I was stunned, but then I saw my brother's coat. It was lying on the chair by the table that was known as "my seat", i.e. that's where Olympia always sat.

Then I understood that something ugly was going on and I decided to call my Mom to make her call off this insanity. If I called the police Robbie might never leave jail again and I hated to do that to the family.

My Mom sounded very strange and I understood at once that this, whatever it was and I could only guess, was her idea. In her foggy condition she had decided that Olympia was rich so she had to pay her crack. I just said something nonsensical about having lost a glove when visiting her. She didn't sound like she believed me, but we left it at that. I stood for some seconds, thinking of phoning the police, but couldn't make myself do it. Then I went to look for Olympia. To find her was quite easy as I followed her blood on the floor.

I soon saw that she must be in her office, but to get there meant walking a creaking staircase. Robbie would hear that so I decided not to walk, but to run up the stairs. Before doing so I found a knife in the kitchen for my protection.

As soon as I set foot on the stairs I heard Robbie: "Hey, Sis, is that you?" I didn't answer, but burst in on them in the office. As soon as I got inside and saw the first glimpse of Olympia, pale and bleeding, but looking as fierce as a Bulldog in the face I received a blow to my head and fell to the floor.

When I woke up I saw my most stupid brother, Stephen, standing by Olympia while Robbie stood by me, holding his knife to my thumb. Olympia was very upset, and she even offered her second thumb to save mine.

I was tied up with my hands in front of me and I couldn't do anything to free myself, let alone helping Olympia, who by the way wasn't tied up. Oh, how I regretted not having phoned the police, but those hooligans were family, and I couldn't bring myself to turn them in. That is, now I could bring myself to do anything, only I didn't know how. When my eye caught the sad sight of Oscar, Olympia's dog, lying dead and bloodied it felt awful. To kill this small, trusting animal was so not acceptable.

We didn't talk, none of us said anything, but suddenly I felt a sharp pain in my thumb and I saw the blood trickle down my slacks. I couldn't help myself, but let out a muffled cry. Olympia started to yell at my brothers: "You swine, you Nazis, you Hitler-sons, stop that, let her go. She doesn't have money ..."

"All right," Robbie said, "but you have loads of money ..." When she didn't answer he cut me once more and then something quite unexpected happened: My fragile and hypochondric grandmother dived into her purse by the desk, quick as lightening she whipped out a gun - and then she shot my brother Stephen. Robbie let out a cry with surprise. She looked at him, head askance, and then she shot him too.

I was so surprised that I can't tell about it. How did this happen? How did all of this happen - the dog, the thumbs, my brothers - all of it was like out of a nightmare, but the pain in my hand convinced me that it was real.

"Granny!" I said, "They are dead! You shot them!"

"Yes," she said, and I'm sorry for you, but those were a couple of bad boys. Let's get the police and then go to the hospital to save your poor thumb ..." By now she was standing by me, cutting the rope they had tied me up with.

"And yours," I said.

"Too late, but never mind, I can use the other hand to shoot."

"Yes," I said, quite awed, "However, did you learn to shoot like that?"

"I should have told you before," she said, "but your late grandfather, my beloved husband, was the best gangster and hit man of our time ..."

"What??!!" I screamt, "What are you talking about, wasn't he a school teacher?"

"Yes, and a damn good one, he taught me everything I know about guns ..."

Even though my hand hurt I couldn't help laughing at my grandfather, this presumed pillar of society, being a gangster, and so did she, in a low, horse cackle.

# The Toad Adventure

Only very few people have ever seen him. Many have heard of him and some just adore him from the cartoons, but basically he is for kids. They like this clumsy and criminal troll. Grown Ups buy the dolls made over his character and give it to their kids, but they don't buy the Toad-ashtrays, the booklets, etc. for themselves. No, he is not popular with grown-ups and why should he be, after all he is a menace in adult company.

When I saw him the first time I recognized him at once: This was Toad, but what was he doing in my brother's garden? Why did he stand next to the roses with an axe in his hand and why was he grinning at me? "Hello!" I shouted, "Who are you and what are you doing in that rose bed?" He just waved at me, then he swung his axe high in the air and let it fall to cut down my favorites in that garden: The roses!

The wonderful, perfect flowers fell like soldiers in World War I. I couldn't help myself, but gave out a "yelp" in disgust. "Toad, how could you?!!!!"

"Aha, now you know me, so you admit that now?"

"What do you mean," I said terrified when I saw him move over to the pear tree, another of my favourites in the garden. He didn't answer, but lifted the axe and gave the defenceless tree a blow that went into my mind and body as were it directed at me. "No-no, please, stop it, Toad," I cried.

"Do you know me or don't you know me?"

"I know you as a character in a cartoon and as a doll ..."

"What," he yelled, obviously disgusted at such a description, "what did you just say?"

"I know you ..."

" ... from a cartoon and as a doll?"

"Yes," I whispered, horrified at the thought of offending him.

"I never was a doll," he said and I dared not even look at the stitches where his doll body was sown together. Instead I gave a half-nod-half-shake of my spinning head that might mean anything.

"Do you admit that I have a good cause to come to see you now that you're grown-up?"

"Mjnah," I answered, again horrified at him for his fierce looks.

"You promised to be my wife when you grew up - and now you are just that: A grown-up, and very pretty, young lady ...."

"I never ..."

"Yes, you did and we even made a contract. If you look into your purse you'll find a copy of it."

"How did it get there?" I asked, quite bewildered.

"It flew into it when I told it to do so ... what else?"

With shaky fingers I opened my purse and took out a crumbled paper I didn't remember that I had seen before. It read: "I, Anna, hereby commit myself to marry Toad right now, only we wait to do so until I'm grown-up." The signature was mine from when I was 7 or 8 years old. I turned the paper and looked at a lot of photos that were glued to it. They made me blush because in all of them this much younger me was kissing Toad in the shape of a 12-13 years old boy.

"You cheated me!" I shouted, now enraged.

"Yes," he said in that special Toad-way that made grown-ups hate him and kids love him. "I did, didn't I? Well, I'm glad I did because you sure has grown into a most delectable, young lady."

"I can't marry a cartoon character. How would our kids look?"

The mentioning of kids made him look sheepish and rather naughty. "No!" I yelled, "that can't be legal. I was 5 or 6 years old."

"Seven," he said with a smile, "and it is - in Cartoon Country. Besides, you've misunderstood the sayings. We already ARE married. Your Teddy Pooh-Pooh saw to it ..."

"But he was a toy, not a human being. Besides, we aren't in Cartoon Country, we are in my world as a human being."

"Interesting," he said, suddenly looking very happy. "Well, then we had better hurry away from here, haven't we, dear wife?" That said, he jumped the 6-7 metres from the pear tree to the spot where I was standing. He swept me up into his arms and kissed me right on the kisser before we set off in the direction of the dark shadows. Somewhere over there I remembered what laid beyond those shadows and I couldn't help smiling and also laugh out at the memory. One thing was for sure, Toad had always been fun to be with and he had always made me laugh. Besides, in Cartoon Country I might easily get a divorce. Thinking this I happened to look down my arms and I understood the situation better because now I saw what I had seen in Toad: They were turning into dolls' arms, stitches and all. The same change was visible in my legs, stitches everywhere. I dared not think of how my new dolls' face looked ...

# A Ghostly Affair

I never liked being passed over as if nobody saw me and now I literally am invisible. All I have in this world is a space of nothingness, a non-form, a nonentity. Well, some - a few living individuals, like e.g. pets, babies and specially gifted, dying or just very old, demented people - may still see me. As to ghosts I haven't met any, except as a passing shadow now and then, but that's OK with me as I still have this contact with the living although they don't know what I am. Should they tell someone about this strange lady, floating through air, these people wouldn't believe them. "A lady, all in grey, who can hover wherever she choses is visiting you all the time? That's nice, hon' ... Such a strange dream, nothing to worry about."

Well, those parents, relatives, doctors, nurses or whatever may be right or they may be wrong as to the worrying part of it. Actually, I'm not too sure myself about this mysterious game called "life after death" .... hmm - well anyway, riddle upon riddle .... I shall learn, no doubt about it, but it's not as fun as I would have thought some time ago when I couldn't do this. Especially the repetitions of highlights from my life is a tiresome game.

For instance the murder scene. Yes, I murdered him, and yes, I used a knife, cutting and stabbing him 27 times. I don't deny it so why do I have to see it repeated over and over again? What is the use of that repetition when they don't repeat my own death. HOW did I die, was I murdered or was it an accident? It can't have been an illness as I was quite young and healthy, but all of a sudden I was in this state of invisibility. Very strange and very unpleasant.

In his moment of death Professor Ethan Hulk all of a sudden looked like the wise, old man he might have become in the 50-60 years I robbed him of. Wonder whether I gained the same facial expression of wisdom as he did when I was murdered - or whatever I was - two weeks later. Somehow I doubt it as I'm not a highly intelligent professor loose-pants at the Science Department at a famous university. No, far from it, but when I killed him I turned into a queen, the one in power and he, the king, turned into nothing but a pig, fit for slaughter.

I told all this to some of those who saw me after I died, but of course, a small baby of 6 months or a demented, old lady of 90 years doesn't understand anything of it. The small baby started to smile and giggle happily when I showed him how I had stabbed the professor and blood had splashed all over. As to the old lady she all of a sudden seemed to understand what I showed her and she didn't like it. She looked positively unhappy for a moment, until she forgot and went back to her senile happiness.

The third one of those I appeared to was an old lover of mine. He got so scared at seeing me that I dissolved back into the grey mist I am dressed in most of the time, but before doing that I caught sight of some clippings on his desk: "Jet-set-queen dead", "Famous, little, rich girl found dead" and so on. All of them with the famous photo of me in an unmistakably erotic position with teenage idol CD. (As if I hadn't done anything except that. Why didn't they bring photos of me together with those people for save-the-animals-societies instead? Oh no, they must show me as the party goose all the time).

The fourth one I approached is a wonderful, but unfortunately very sick, young girl, Anette. She suffers from cancer and I can't imagine that she is going to survive for long. However, she is a fighter so who knows? Not I as one thing is for sure: The longer I've been dead the less I know. Strange as I used to think I knew everything ....

Well, Anette sees me clearly and she accepts me fully. "Hello Ghoasty!" she whispers when I come: "Nice seeing you. Been killing someone lately?"

"Oh, you naughty brat," I joke back at her, "I might kill you ..."

Her smile grows sad and had I been solid I might have kicked myself for such a stupid remark to a dying friend.

"OK," she says, "but no knives."

"No," that was solely for Professor "Down-with-your-pants-and-bend-over"."

"As long as he didn't rape them ..."

"But that's the point, he did, because had they not given in to him he would have flunked them. That's what happened to my little sister Bev'."

At my mentioning of Bev' she grew silent for a while. This had happened several times lately and I wondered why, but didn't want to ask her. After a little while she said: "Even so, to kill a man over ..."

"Rape? It more than suffices and he did so much more."

"Suffering from a brain tumour doesn't help my memory, so could you tell me once more ..."

"OK," I said, "I had heard about him for ages, and I knew what he did to girls and women. When Bev' told me that he had flunked her for refusing to sleep with him I went to see him and then that damn creature attacked me, trying to rape me. We fought and I got more and more angry - then I took out my knife which I had brought for protection and he started to laugh at me. What he didn't know was that I've been a fencer for years. I've even won several contests so he was an easy prey for me."

"And then you died yourself?"

"Not until two weeks after the ... incident."

"I've made my brother find some obituaries for you and also some articles. It seems that you died in an accident."

"I wasn't murdered?" I really was surprised as many have threatened to kill me over the years, actually both Bev' and some ex-boyfriends.

"You tumbled down the stairs, broke your neck and died."

"Strange! I was quite agile, didn't trip over my own feet or so."

"I think you should start meditating, perhaps you will be able to see what happened. Actually, you might do it right now as I need to sleep for a while."

"Meditate? All right, I haven't done it for a long time, but I know how." As Anette closed her eyes and soon dozed off I sat down to meditate which is a strange thing to do for ghosts, but I soon got the knack of it and before long I saw an inner image of myself standing on top of that staircase. I also saw two beautifully manicured women's hands give me one push in my back. At once I stumbled and fell, tumbling down, down and down the numerous steps and landing in an awkward position at the foot of the stairs. Obviously I was dead.

When Anette woke up I told her about the women's hands. "Didn't that woman wear a ring, a bracelet or something else which you might recognize her be?"

"I don't think so ..." I answered, but then an image of a hand appeared in my mind: "Yes, by God, it's Bev'!! But why?"

Anette nodded once. She didn't look surprised which came as a shock to me. "Because you killed her dream boy."

"What?!! I yelled, "I took out a rapist, a bad guy ..."

"Whom she was trying to change into a nice and loving ... husband, that's why she turned him down. She wanted to appear as wife material by not behaving like all the others giving in to him. Well, he never took the bait, but she was still hoping that he would when you stepped in and killed him."

I sat totally still for a while, stunned by the plausibility in what she said. "Bev' couldn't have done that ..."

Anette smiled: "Well, actually she told me herself."

"You don't know her!"

"I do now ... after she became ... hm, what you are ..."

"What?!!!"

"Yes," she died in a drowning accident last week, but she is a bit shy over what she did to you so you haven't met yet."

This was so overwhelming that I set off, took a few rounds above her bed and then went back to sit at it. "This is too much," I said.

"Yes, it might be called "irony" or "craziness", if you chose ... Do you want to see Bev'?"

I thought the matter over for some minutes and then said: "No! She made me believe that he had wronged her, she both used me and she killed me. We shall meet, but not now. - By the way, have you seen him too?"

"No, he isn't here, maybe he went to Hell ..."

"My life - and my death - is a farce, but I can't laugh at it, it's also too tragic." If I had had tears I would have shed them.

Anette said: "Perhaps I shall join you when I die."

"Don't talk like that, you are too young to die."

"So were you and who knows, that ghoastly thing may be fun when one gets to know it better. Bev' seems to enjoy herself much more than you do."

"Figures," I said bitterly, but looking at her emaciated face and now very deep-set eyes I knew that she was right and that this "life" held some possibilities I hadn't thought of. To my own dismay I suddenly felt like laughing at the absurdity of the situation. "OK," I said, "I shall become "The Merry Ghost of the Staircase"."

"Better, "The Merry Ghost of the World" as the world is much more than one staircase not worth haunting ..." I looked at her and burst out laughing as did she.

# The Tell-Tale Notes:

This long, winding staircase was more than she could climb. She stood looking up at it and felt her heart sink into her shoes, already brim full with her swollen feet. - Oh, she exclaimed, turning around and looking appealingly at her son.

- All right, he said, a little annoyance in his voice, I shall get it for you. Then he started to climb the stairs, his big frame making it creak at each step. She felt exited, hopeful and at the same time resigned to the message she expected to have from up there where he was now, looking at all the binders with papers, pictures and clippings.

- Here it is, he exclaimed and started back down to her. Three binders. How heavy they are, he said, annoyance in his well moduled voice. His civilization-organ she had called it as it was such a polite and schooled voice, trained to impress voters and journalists.

- Come, she said, pulling his sleeve, let's go to the table and have a look. They cleared a corner of the large table, now littered with papers and scraps of papers. - This is so exciting.

He smiled at her eager face and hurriedly opened one of the binders. - Hm, strange, a lot of envelopes, closed and sealed ... It looks very private indeed.

- Never mind, she said merrily, never mind, he is dead now and all of it belongs to us. She started to tear at the lock of one of the other binders. It was obviously old, but the lock looked new. Like our marriage, she thought. Old meets young ...

The lock gave way and she saw a lot of closed envelopes. - There are some here too, she said, very surprised and a little annoyed. - Well, let's open them.

He didn't look happy at the thouoght. - I think we should bring them to Mr. Caribbean, after all he was his lawyer.

- Mr. Caribbean is a good lawyer, but I was married to your father and night after night I saw him sitting there, browsing his binders without ever telling me what they were about. I want to open those envelopes.

- And if we find something you'll not like?

- I never found anything in that relationship I did like ...

He looked sad and hurt when she said it. - Except you, of course. You were the gem he gave me. But now I want to see those envelopes.

- OK, let's open one each ... He tore at the paper, and then turned the envelope upside-down. Out fell 4-5 photoes, a small tape and a few other objects. She dashed for the photoes, but had to turn them over several times on the table before she realized what they were. Then she let out a sigh and fell to a sloping posture in her chair. He took the photoes from her hand and at first glance he let out a: "Damn creature. How I hate him!"

Her eyes filled with tears, but then she started to tear at another envelope. When it gave way, out fell a small heap of photoes, a tape and a lady's wristwatch. This time she didn't reveal any emotions, just slammed the emptied envelope down on the table with its former contents.

Mother and son sat back, their eyes locking across the binders, the full envelopes and the emptied ones. - And this you wanted to give to the lawyer .... Oh, what are we to do?

Her son's eyes had grown narrow, but also very thoughtful. - I shall never accept to let anyone in on this secret, he said, I have a family and I have a career ...

- Yes, and so had he, she said bitterly. She raised her hand when she saw him ready to talk. He was my husband, our marriage wasn't easy which you know, but I loved him when we married. What he felt I have no idea of, but I honor my own young love. Also, he was your father, from seeing these photoes I wish he wasn't, but that's neither here nor there.

- What do you suggest?
- To destroy all this ...
- But what about the families of these young, missing girls? Shouldn't they know that they are dead and that the murderer is known?
- No, and as you said, you've a family now, should your kids know what kind of a man their grandfather was?

He sat silent for a while. - What about opening all these envelopes, collect the photoes that tell of their death and get them to the police?

She didn't answer, but sat back in her chair and let her eye scan all the shelves of the library. Suddenly she caught sight of the large full body painting of him in a riding dress, whip in hand. She rose to her feet and went over to have a closer look. His beautiful eyes stared at her from the painting, his handsome looks always made an impression on her, and this time it annoyed her. She bent forward so her face was close to his and then she let herself sink into his eyes. Darkness was what she saw, darkness beyond brown which were the true colour of those eyes. It engulfed her and when she lifted her head, tearing herself away from him, she knew her son was right.

- Yes, she said, they should know, but how?

- I fear they shall find out from the furniture where the torture is, but it must be done. If my Sophie disappeared for years I would want to know ...

- The furniture? Oh, it's gone, the weekend cottage burnt down five years ago, when he wasn't as agile as he had been.

They started to open and browse all the envelopes, then they chose all those that were of the final moments in many, many young women's lives. After doing that they put them into one large envelope, sealed it and then they found a London police station on the map. - This one, she said, turning once more to look at the painting. She felt that those eyes had changed from the darkest black into the colour of the sea when it mirrors the approaching storm.

# Foreboding

At first she didn't know what it was, that feeling, that sense like a vague memory of the smell of spilled liquids. Then it dawned upon her that she had felt like this before and every time it happened something proved to be different from what it was supposed to be. When she realized this she was gripped by those strange reflexes that bid her to straighten her back and stand as tall as she could. Her nostrils were flaunting like on a horse, ready to flee, her heart was pounding, almost to the point of suffocating her. Yes, this was a foreboding, something out there told her something about her situation inside the room.

- No sounds, she thought to herself and felt relief at this seeming proof that there wasn't anything out there, but then she caught sight of the landlord's cat, lying on her bed and then she knew that the place wasn't without sounds. On the contrary, it was full of them, only not for her poor ears. - Bagpuss knows more than me, she thought, his ears are with the sounds, but his eyes are with me. She grew cold and shuddered when realizing that the cat was staring at her, at the same time fully attent upon the sounds she couldn't hear.

She went over to the bed and patted the grey, old head of the animal, ignoring the malicious, yellow eyes staring at her, until they all of a sudden closed, blotting out their lantern quality of curiosity. A dull, sonorous sound arose from its breast, telling her of cat pleasures in being fondled, but still his alertness was on. The ears picked up every sound in the house.

- What's going on? she asked herself, looking at the drowsy animal laying there motionless except for the eyelids which fluttered as if it was dreaming very interesting, predatory dreams. - Oh, you lazy, old cat she said with a sigh and went over to the window to scan the street outside from behind the curtains. To her horror she saw the younger brother of the landlord as he stepped out from the back door to the house and started to walk up the garden path to the front door.

- Billy, oh no, she exclaimed and hurried to the door to turn the key and put on the brand new safety chain. Also she pulled a chair up to the door and set it up against it.

- Damn! she said out loud, suddenly feeling the need of hearing a human voice in the room. - Damn, damn, damn!

She picked up the phone, but it was dead in her hand. No sound, no feeling of life in the small, black thingy which she knew was outmoded.

- Why aren't you a cell phone, she almost yelled into it's black deafness, perfectly aware that the only reason it wasn't more functional was her own lack of wish to pay the money to have another one which couldn't get disconnected by anyone but her.

- You always behave like you're so poor, Billy had sneered at her that awful time when he had first forced his way into her room, but you're not. Your nephew told me, you're rich, might live somewhere else and still be rich.

- How could he say something like that, she thought. How?! She was poor and the money she inherited she couldn't touch out of respect for the deceased, he knew that, but he was evil, always forcing himself upon her, either for "love" or for money. And she, being what she was, didn't dare do anything, not even flee, no, nothing ...

A muffled sound from the hall told her that by now he was inside the house. She put her ear to the door and heard how he tried to open it with the old keys. She laughed a muted laugh to herself at the thought that he still believed he had the key to her room. - Oh no, she said under her breath, not this time, new key, new rules ...

She realized that the cat had come and that it sat beside her, staring at the door, yellow-eyed and very alert. - What is it, she whispered down toward the pointed ears. It looked up at her and then let out a "Meow" that made her jump because of its suddenness and because she knew that the sound gave her away to the man outside the door. - No, she whispered, no, shut up ...

Billy's voice penetrated the door. - Hey, you old hag, open the door NOW.

- Go away, she stutterered, her voice shaking like she was herself. Go away, this is my room, you have no right ...

He laughed and punched the door so the chair in front of it literally jumped.

- Oldie-Goldie, he sneered, little, rich hag, give me your bag or I shall take it myself ...

She felt how the tears filled her eyes, but she forced back the sobbing in her throat. - You can't get in, so stay away ...

Then once again she felt the cat against her legs and looked down at it. The ears, the pointed ears listened to something, no doubt about it and suddenly she knew what it was. It was the muffled sound of screws being unscrewed, of boards being lifted and removed, of some tools doing a wonderful job at getting the sinister, young man the access he wanted.

*Else Cederborg*

Also she knew that there was nothing she could do about it, but that she simply couldn't give him the fortune that she to her surprise had inherited from her elusive and unknown father and had hoarded ever since, ready to give it back to the dead man who had wanted to secure the future of this illegitimate daughter, but who only succeeded in creating a Hell for her.

## Gangsters And Animals:

Once there was a young girl who lived in poverty because her family was poor. However, she had great plans for her future because she was a BEAUTY. Not many are as beautiful as she was and she knew that this might be a useful key to another world.

All she had to do was to find "Mr. Right" - i.e. "Mr. Loaded" - and that she considered an easy part of her plans. She felt that somewhere out there among all the rich people of this world Mr. Right was looking for HER and nobody else.

Well, as we know fate is a tease so when she did find someone who resembled her Mr. Right what she found was a Mr. Fake out to find his Miss Loaded. The outcome of this was an awful, abusive marriage and one daughter who was even prettier than her pretty Mom. After some fightings - even in public - the spouses divorced, each feeling cheated beyond words.

The daughter, Charlotte, wasn't only the most beautiful girl in the world, she was also a good soul, kind to people and animals. Also she didn't feel pretty, although her Mom often told her that she was and that "out there Mr. Right/Loaded was waiting for her". It didn't mean a thing to her, and she wasn't even looking for a Mr. Right - rich or not - all she wanted was to qualify to become a vet so that she could help saving the not-so-endearing animals of this world. She had an idea about how she could make poisonous animals popular with people who abhorred everything not furry and cuddly. It really made her sad to see how people didn't take to ugly or dangerous animals and she often had cried over flattened toads and snakes.

She was a member of an organisation for helping animals of all kinds and she almost always had some little animal patient or foster child to care for. Sometimes she had to take the animals to the vet of the organisation, a nerdy, young man, Geoffrey, who quite often looked a little like a sleep-walker. Actually, he might be as he had a knack of spending the night in front of his computer. Just like Charlotte he had no idea of his looks. Had someone asked him the colour of his eyes he wouldn't have been able to answer such a question, but he knew that the girls didn't look at him twice. He, on the other hand, often looked at girls, especially Charlotte, whose extraordinary looks had set something inside him in the highest state of alert, only he didn't know that that was what non-nerds call "falling in love", although he wasn't quite without experiences of a carnal nature. All he knew was that he liked to be with her and had a strong urge to kiss her, but didn't dare to make the first move.

When Charlotte came to see him over a sick sparrow that she had befriended he nearly forgot his obligations as a vet over her beauty. Rather embarassing actually, but she didn't notice anything unusual in this awkward, young man whom she never had looked at twice.

"I think he has a broken wing," she said, looking both pretty and worried. "He can't lift the right one, only the left one."

Geoffrey conducted the most thorough examination that any young sparrow has experienced in the hands of a young vet. Had Charlotte been aware of her own looks she wouldn't have leaned forward so it looked like she was offering him a glimpse of her exquisite bosom, but in her concern for the sparrow (which she called Henry) she was even more unconscious of her looks than she used to be.

Poor, nerdy Geoffrey mistook this and some other unconscious exhibits of loveliness as some conscious attempts to entice him. Charlotte couldn't have been more surprised had she known because she had no feelings for him whatsoever. That is, sometimes when he handled the animals in a very tender and expert manner she did feel a sort of sting in her breast, but nothing could have induced her to see this as more than admiration for his skills. After having grown up being told over and over, day by day, how beautiful she was and how that rich Mr. Right was waiting for her she secretly abhorred the falling-in-love-game, but especially the secret look-good-contests that were second nature to her mother.

After tending to the sparrow Geoffrey had seen enough of the lovelinesses of Charlotte to feel that she must be interested in him and would accept an invite for a date. Charlotte got so surprised that she said "yes" before she had had time to think the matter over. Besides, to her a date with Geoffrey wasn't anything but a chance of discussing animals with the vet.

The day of the date he took her to a diner. He had never been there, but the name of the place appealed to him: "Paradiso". Unfortunately this was anything but Paradise. The food was awful, and all the others, guests and servants alike, looked like movie-gangsters. Charlotte didn't like the food, and she was surprised at the place itself, but having the opportunity of discussing animals she felt that the evening wasn't quite wasted.

That is, until the nephew of the propriotor, Salvatore II, saw her and made a bee dive for her. He sat down at the table next to her and Geoffrey, trying to engage her in a conversation, all the time extolling her looks. He spoke in a manner she wasn't used to and she was shocked at the rudeness of his compliments. She made it clear to Geoffrey that she wanted to leave and he hurriedly paid the bill. That surprised and angered Salvatore II as this was his usual way to talk to women. He found it charming to call them "dolls" and the like. To him that was a compliment, but to Charlotte it was an affront.

When she and Geoffrey sat in his car she was very quiet. Then she noticed that Salvatore II was right behind them in his fast sports car and she got scared. "Don't bring me home now," she said, "let's drive a little to get him off the track." Geoffrey found this ruse very wise indeed, and he drove out of town. However, it soon became clear to him that Salvatore II wasn't easy to get rid of. At one point he drove up beside Geoffrey's car and shouted at the couple that he wanted to talk to them. Geoffrey tried to look like he didn't hear him and Charlotte frowned at him, but Salvatore II didn't stop. He followed close by in their tracks, i.e. until something happened: A car coming from the other direction hit him full front. The impact was such as to leave out any doubts about survivals of either of the drivers.

"What are we to do?" Charlotte asked.

"That depends on you," Geoffrey answered. "Shall we report it and tell the police everything that happened or shall we leave and phone them anonymously?"

Charlotte suddenly remembered the colourful compliments not only of Salvatore II, but of his cousins, Luigi and Fabrizio, and she didn't like the looks of it. She was afraid to become a target for the entire family, both over her looks and over her part in the accident. "Let's drive and report it anonymously," she said, not looking at Geoffrey as she was ashamed of her decision. It didn't feel right, but still, she felt it to be necessary.

After having done what they had planned they sat talking in the car for a while and it felt quite natural to both of them that Geoffrey at some point took her in his arms and kissed her. Actually, she might have kissed him if he hadn't made the first move, as she needed the feel of reassurance and consolation after all the events of the evening. Not once did she feel like talking of animals and pets, but the subject of suspect gangster-look-alikes was at the tip of her tongue. Before long she succumbed to her need and brought it up. He told her, as was the truth, that he didn't know this family and that he had chosen the diner from the name. She found that kind of funny and also touching. After kissing once more they took goodbye for the evening and she went inside her mother's house.

The very next morning she received the first of in all 11 parcels with dead animals. It was a shock to her to open one of these parcels and find a murdered animal and she phoned Geoffrey at once. He hadn't received anything, he said, and neither did he when she got the next one. However, now they met regularly, discussing what to do in this situation of implicit threats. Geoffrey was much for "sticking together" as he put it and so they did. Psychologically Charlotte got very dependent on him - that is until one early morning when she was up and haphazardly looked out the window: There she saw the well-known figure of Geoffrey carrying a small parcel which he put at the door of her mother's house.

She at once saw that this parcel was like the others she had received, by post or by messenger. When he had gone she tiptoed down, got the parcel and opened it: Inside she found the dead body of her sparrow friend, Henry, and it was obvious to her that his neck had been broken. Somehow she wasn't really surprised, but she was sad for Henry who had been full of lust for life and who now had become the victim of a man who thought that fright for the gangsters's revenge would keep her by his side.

She sat down, grabbed her cell phone and phoned Geoffrey. He sounded very happy at hearing her voice, until he realized what she was saying: "I liked Henry, and I also liked you, but now I've lost both of you. Don't ever come near me again or I shall revisit "Paradiso" and have a talk with those cousins of Salvatore II. After all they can't be as dangerous as you are ..."

# Suspended in Midair

Catherine didn't want to attend the morning table. She told her maid, Suzanne, that she didn't feel well, that she had a headache and had decided to stay in her rooms. Suzanne sent her mistress a noncommital glance. Actually, the expression of her face went from sulky housemaid to "Mask of A Goddess of Contempt".

As it was Catherine didn't blame her because she knew that as a maid she had to work at all hours and that her pay was very small. That was the life of the housemaid in the 1890'ies just as it was the life of the daughter of a wealthy house to be weak and sickly. Paleness was the goal, tanned skin the threat to someone like herself who had to look her rôle in society: The tender and not exactly robust lily.

Five minutes after she had told Suzanne that she wouldn't come down for breakfast her mother came to see her. "Now, what is this, Cat?" she said in an annoyed voice.

"I'm not feeling well," Catherine answered. "I don't sleep that well at the moment and I've got a headache."

"Not now, you promised me ..."

Catherine shot a glance at her mother, then she lowered her head and stared into her lap.

"You know who is coming ... and why ..."

Catherine felt how she blushed, but she didn't speak.

"It's important that you show yourself ..."

"Then he shall see that I'm not the right wife for him, as sickly and weak as I am. After all he himself has fought lions and tigers, rebels and murderers in Africa."

"There are no tigers in Africa," her mother said, impatiently, "but you simply have to show up, no matter what. I shall send Suzanne to help you with the green dress."

"Green dress in the morning?!"

"Yes, and I hope it makes a good impression because this is your chance in life."

Catherine understood her only too well. Being the eldest of five sisters her parents had to find a husband to her so that her four younger sisters might have their chance in life, i.e. to get married.

Five minutes later Catherine went downstairs in her beautiful green dress. As she stepped into the dining-room she saw at once the man who might ask for her hand this morning. They had never set eyes on each others, but her mother had corresponded with his mother and this morning-meeting had been set up by these two dragons of society because he was to leave for business abroad that same day.

Suzanne was close by and Catherine felt reassured by her maid, simply because they were the same age. Had she been able to see her close behind her back she would have realized that she and her maid caught sight of Mr. Santini at the exact same moment. Whereas she lowered her eyes and looked the picture of the well-brought-up and thus demure daughter of a good family the eyes of the maid and the man interlocked for some seconds more than was quite proper.

The eyes whom Catherine met had a certain glint to them. Somehow they were very attractive indeed, but also they were frightening. This handsome man was no puppy dog and although Catherine didn't know much about human character she sensed that quality in him. She was dumbfounded at seeing this handsome and attractive man as her suitor. From what she had heard her friends talking about it was very common to marry off very young girls to middle-aged or even old men and that was what she had expected to meet this morning, but he was neither. Being 25 years she was considered old, but being a man he was young with his 32 years of age.

The morning went by like after a ruler. They had breakfast, they talked and they got engaged! The last part of it was taken care of by her father - exasperated by all those daughters - and Mr. Santini who seemed eager to settle down and start a family. Catherine felt the passenger on a mad roller-coaster, she didn't like this haste and at the same time she felt relieved by it. The dice were cast, now it was up to Fate ...

When Mr. Santini came back from his trip to tend business abroad they were married right away and after a short honeymoon in France he whisked her off to his house in the country. She was glad to have Suzanne with her. The wedding and the start of married life had been too much for her, never had she expected what was part of being married and never would she have known that she was pregnant had it not been for her. Her maid wheeled herself into her confidence because her mother, sisters and aunts were far away. Besides, right now all the women of the family were busy arranging the wedding of the next one of her sisters. By now two others were engaged to get married, only one hadn't had any suitors and although Catherine felt ashamed and abused by the intimacies of married life she also felt sorry for this her youngest sister who was left unengaged as some kind of misfit.

As she grew bigger her husband left her alone. He was very satisfied that he would soon be the father of a son - he never considered the possibility that the child might be a daughter - and treated his wife with much respect.

To Catherine this was a relief, and it also gave her time to start observing her surroundings in a more detailed manner. She went on small expeditions in the large house and one day she found a locked door that none of her keys was able to open. The door became an obsession with her and she tried everything she could to open it, except breaking it down. All in vain until one day the door suddenly was open. As she went in she saw a strange rope-contraption in the ceiling and the walls, something looking like a tool for exercising. Next time the door was open she found some clothes on the floor, and now she started to brood about this strange thing. - What could it be? And the clothes looked strange, torn and bloody as they were. She knew better than to ask her husband or Suzanne, but she wondered at her find. Also she wondered at muffled sounds in the night. It sounded like woeful whimperings, but she ended up putting it down to the wind.

One morning she wasn't attended by Suzanne as she was supposed to be. She sent for the cook, whom she felt was her friend, and asked her to go to see what was wrong. When she came back she was told that Suzanne was down with the flu and was afraid to pass it on to her mistress in her tender situation, now that the baby might be due at any moment. The cook had a very strange and bewildered expression on her face when she told her mistress these news, but she saw to it that the youngest parlormaid came to help her. After being dressed by her Suzanne set out on her house inspection, instinctively aiming for the mystery-room. This time she found both clothes and blood on the floor. Staring at her find she could hardly take it in. What was going on in this house? She was the mistress of it and she didn't know the first things about it. This was not right! She felt betrayed, but didn't know by whom except that it went far back in time. The faces of her parents flashed by and then her husband, all of them were traitors, she knew that now, but had nothing to set up against it. As an afterthought the pretty and haughty face of Suzanne also flashed by her inner eye, but that she felt was unfair.

After making her husband the happiest father to the baby boy he had dreamt of she was considered a patient. That gave her more time to inspect the house and she once more set out for the strange room. As she was quite close by she heard muffled sounds within and she froze in her tracks, afraid to be found by those inside the room. Then the muffled sounds suddenly turned into a piercing scream. In a few steps she was at the door and this time it was the knowledge of having been used, of being locked in an unhappy marriage that gave her courage to open the door. She flung it open and nearly tumbled down with surprise at what she saw: Her husband quite nude - which was the first time she saw that - standing, whip in hand, in front of the suspended Suzanne. She was tied down and now hang in midair, ready to be used as he found convenient. Looking at him it was very obvious that that moment was now.

"What!" she exclaimed, but then she caught the cold eyes of her husband as he walked toward her and, without uttering a single word, pushed her outside the door, locking it from within. Standing there, her back to the door, she felt her situation in its full extent. This slave-like life had become hers, but none, absolutely none of it, she had wanted herself. In a way she was in the same position as the by now weeping Suzanne.

# The Brave Woman's Ordeal:

The pain took on rhytms that went like a powerful piston. Something well-known and yet new. As Erica opened her eyes she wondered why this pain filled the world to the brim and why she was hurting. The pain was everywhere, like needles in her back, like deep, almost drill-like pangs all over.

She felt an urge to wipe her hair out of her eyes, but couldn't. The pain crystalized into realization: She couldn't move freely because her limbs were tied to the bedposts.

Desperate she tried to scream, but found herself gagged. The scream that stuck in her throat choked her when it blended with a sudden wild rage. Desperately she wriggled to free her limbs, to remove the underwear that sat in her throat. Then she heard the voice of the man she couldn't see: "That's right, darling. Don't lie there like a lump of dough. You know how, just do it again, hon."

All of a sudden her brain filled with memories and pictures of someone, a man, entering the window of her house, his fist in her face and the blankness that came out of his repeated blows. So this is what it is, she thought to herself, RAPE! With that realization she jagged her head forwards and when she heard his gasp, she knew that she had hit him hard on the nose. Now, it's not only my blood, she thought, before she passed out once more from his enraged blow to her head.

When she came to once again she knew that he was gone, that he had escaped the way he had come and that she still was tied to the bedposts. Now she saw other eyes than his staring at her: Her wonderful, little terrier Susie who looked inquisitively at her. A pity you can't help me, she thought to herself. Susie wagged her tail and stared, but that was all.

Erica knew that if she didn't free herself and get help she might suffocate on the underwear he had jammed into her mouth or the blood trickling down from her sore scalp. Very slowly she let her tongue press out the underwear from her mouth and when her it was free to bite at the rope tyeing her down. It took a while, but as soon as one of her hands was free she found the scissors in her bedside table and then it was a piece of cake to cut off the rope of her other limbs.

Soon after that she dialed 911 and the police came. Before she was taken to the hospital she saw to it that Susie was taken in custody with her neighbour and friend, Anette. At the hospital she was interviewed by a nice, female police officer. However, not being able to remember the face of the assailant she didn't have much hope that he would be brought in. "Are you sure that you saw him, but you forgot his face?"

"Yes," she answered, "I saw him, but I can't remember what he looks like."

The police officer heaved a deep sigh. "All right," she said, "phone me if you remember something more." After this nice lady left her in her hospital bed she started to picture it all to herself. She still didn't see the face of the man, but she sensed him, felt his presence, his personality, not to mention the smell of his poignant cologne. Then she realized that this wasn't memories, no, not the past, but the present. Bewildered, but not scared she opened her eyes to look right into the eyes of the male nursing aide who had come to attend her. The smell of his cologne submerged her in one take and it carried her away when she once again felt his hands on her throat.

"Hello there," nurse Petersen said, smiling wryly. "So you were a clever girl who cut herself loose, were you?" As he held her on the throat with one hand and the mouth with another she couldn't answer him, but tried to nod a "yes". "A bit too clever," he went on, "a real bitch ..."

To her surprise she sensed a deep anger in his voice as if she was the culprit and not he. "You just shut up and keep quiet, or else ... he said, looking very threateningly. At the same time he wipped out a photo from his pocket and showed it to her. To her surprise it was Susie sitting in a car, looking quite content. "What?!" she exclaimed now that he didn't hold her throat anymore. "What is this?"

"It's a dog, your little, annoying toy."

"Yes, I can see that," she exclaimed, "it's Susie."

"Oh is that the name of the beast. Well, never mind, now you know that if you talk then Susie will not get the chance of chewing on any more bones in this life."

Erica felt the tears in her eyes. She hadn't cried for herself, but Susie's predicament made her very unhappy. "What about ...?"

"Your neighbour? A very nice lady, but not able to look after your dog anymore."

She looked at him in horror. What had he done to Anette, she wondered. However she dared not ask him.

To her horror he was once more groping for her, touching her, prying and then stopping with a shrug. "Will have to wait," he said, "too many people here right now."

As he left her room she heaved a sigh of relief, but then she started to plan what to do. The kidnapped dog - and Anette too - tied her hands: She dared not do anything like e.g. phoning that nice police lady. On the other hand, if she didn't do anything he might kill her and, if the others were still alive, them too. Could she phone a friend or what could she?

First of all she decided to send a description of nurse Petersen and of his crimes to her own computer by using her cell phone. That way she had secured her story if she was to perish. Then she let herself slide into the wonderful state of a succesful meditation. That was something she used when she was stressed. When she left that state after 15 minutes of meditations she knew that her only chance was to report this new development to the police. She sent the police lady an email and also a SMS over her cell phone, urging her to come "in disguise", i.e. not dressed in uniform, but pretending to be one of her friends. Also she told her about her fear of Anette and Susie. In the photo of the dog she had seen a tall building which she recognized as the town hall. Maybe the dog was hidden somewhere inside or outside that place.

After having sent the email and the SMS she waited patiently for more than an hour, then she sent all of it once more even though she nearly was caught doing it. Being the patient of her assailant she didn't have much time for herself - and each time he came he started to abuse her - so she really was relieved when the door opened and the police officer returned back, dressed as a civilian.

"I'm sorry it took so long," she said, but we have been very busy --- your friend ..."

"Is she dead?!"

"Yes," I'm sorry, but she was both raped and killed. As to the dog ..."

"Yes?"

"Well, Susie, is doing fine. She is at the station right now, we found her with his mother. Now, she is a nice lady who suspects her son of almost anything ..."

Suddenly there was noises and yellings outside the door. Erica recognized nurse Petersen's voice. He was shouting her name, both appealing to her and threatening her.

"Don't worry," the police lady said, "you shall only meet him once in court. When we examined his flat we found a lot of ladies' clothes, wigs and also natural hair that had been cut off ... Yes, cut off," she repeated. "All of it belonged to women who were raped and murdered. You were lucky, but first and foremost you were clever. Without that you might have been dead now ..."

Erica listened to her voice, which intermingled with the voice of the desperate man being taken off to the station. Somehow these voices resembled a duet from some nightmarish opera ...